The Zombie Rule Book

A Zombie Apocalypse Survival Guide

T0159459

The Zombie Rule Book

A Zombie Apocalypse Survival Guide

Tony Newton

COSMIC
EGG
BOOKS

Winchester, UK
Washington, USA

First published by Cosmic Egg Books, 2014
Cosmic Egg Books is an imprint of John Hunt Publishing Ltd., Laurel House, Station Approach,
Alresford, Hants, SO24 9JH, UK
office1@jhpbooks.net
www.johnhuntpublishing.com

For distributor details and how to order please visit the 'Ordering' section on our website.

Text copyright: Tony Newton 2013

ISBN: 978 1 78279 334 2

A CIP catalogue record for this book is available from the British Library.

Design: Stuart Davies

Printed and bound by CPI Group (UK) Ltd, Croydon, CR0 4YY

We operate a distinctive and ethical publishing philosophy in all
areas of our business, from our global network of authors to
production and worldwide distribution.

Rules and tips for surviving the zombie apocalypse

The following information may save your life.

This book is designed to fit perfectly in your bug-out bag.

The rules in this book should be used only in the event of a zombie outbreak.

This rule book will help you to survive in the event of a zombie apocalypse.

Will you be prepared when the zombie apocalypse strikes.

These rules will turn you into a survivor.

Throughout this book you will learn how to survive in the event of a zombie apocalypse and learn how to be a survivor.

Use the following information to your advantage. Think like a survivor. When the zombie apocalypse descends upon us you will be a few steps ahead of the rest. Read re-read, practice and apply, train hard and always think smart. You are a born survivor.

This book of zombie survival rules will be a great asset to anyone preparing themselves for the zombie apocalypse.

If you are prepared for the zombie apocalypse you are prepared for anything!

The book the living dead don't want you to have!

About the author

Tony Newton is a writer from Essex in the UK. Tony has been writing from a young age. He is a prepper and avid survival enthusiast who enjoys writing a broad range from self-help to fiction.

Disclaimer

All tips, hints and information from within this book are intended for use in the event of the zombie apocalypse. Until then they are for entertainment purposes only. The author will not be held responsible for any loss, damage or injury which has occurred from information within this publication.

Introduction

Zombies........... The un-dead, the walking dead, the living dead, the plague, creepers, walkers, shufflers, flesh eaters, the rising dead, biters, brain eaters, the decayed dead, gravers or even demons. Call them what you will but zombies aren't to be taken lightly, they are your most dangerous enemy. They may be the cause of the end of the world as we know it. We've seen them on the screen in horror movies like, *Night of the Living Dead* and *Dawn of the Dead.* Even in romantic comedies like, *Shaun of the Dead.* We now even have TV shows such as *The Walking Dead.* Watching them for entertainment in the audience of a theatre with a big gulp and a bag of hot butter melted popcorn, or relaxed on the sofa at home, eating another chunk of that huge bar of dairy chocolate is one thing. But it's a whole different ball game to come face to face with these evil beings; these death-walking creepers who have only one thing on their mind and that is to eat your flesh. Unless you want to end up as zombie feed then learn these rules now. Just look at the news, it is time to prepare yourself!

Imagine turning on the TV or radio or looking out the window to see flesh-eating zombies everywhere. A virus is spreading hour by hour, minute by minute, at a rate that no other virus in history has ever done before. If you where not prepared you would have no chance of survival. Maybe if you had luck on your side you might survive a few days, only to end up with no shelter, food or water, walking into a horde of zombies and wishing you had died with the ones you left behind. Now imagine if you were prepared, you knew exactly what to do in the event of the zombie apocalypse; where to go, what to take with you, how to react when face to face with zombies and rogue survivors. You knew what plants are safe to eat when you are hungry and miles from anywhere. You knew how to make a shelter and survive. If you want to learn how to survive, keep reading.

The word zombie originated from Haitian folk-lore and is normally associated with voodoo zombies. Irish zombies, or most commonly, Haiti zombies have been mentioned in folk-lore for hundreds of years. The zombies we are talking about dealing with here are the dead, who have come back to life in what looks like a living state (albeit very different from a normal living state) caused by a virus, contamination or even radiation. These zombies contrary to books and films do not have the ability to use weapons and are not highly intelligent but will do all they can to devour your flesh. Zombies can bite, scratch and even transmit infection from their nails. They can grab hold of skin, bone or even clothing whilst trying to feed. Like a dog with a bone between its paws. You won't see a dog holding the TV remote control in its clutches but when it comes to holding a bloody, meaty bone the dog will be firmly grasping it for ease of feasting. A zombie would react in the same way.

A single zombie is bad enough but when they are together in hordes they are nothing short of a nightmare to escape from. Be sure never to enter into a situation in which you will be stuck in the middle of a horde of zombies, the chances are you will not escape unless you have a large group with you, with hundreds of rounds of ammunition, a machine gun and a large degree of luck on your side.

A zombie is dead, but has risen from the grave or has bitten a living human being, not instantly killing the victim, but instead infecting them. The victim will normally pass out or just grow weaker and weaker from the virus until the human body doesn't have the strength to tolerate it. The time will vary with each individual. After this the victim's body will jolt back to what appears to the human eye as a living state but there will be noticeable differences. The eyes will be bloodshot and veins throughout their bodies will be prominent. Even if the victim has lost a limb or has bullet wounds it will still be able to walk. If the zombie has lost its legs it will be able to crawl and drag itself to feed. Zombies feed on human flesh, they will attack any part of the human body, and they seem to have a favourite part of the body which is the brain for reasons unknown. They will devour flesh down to the bone. Zombies can only be killed by totally destroying the brain and in certain cases even a decapitated head is still a major threat; it can still bite. The zombie virus is very infectious and when it strikes will spread faster than any other strain of flu or any other virus in history.

As frightening as an asteroid strike, global financial collapse, solar flare, a pandemic that is natural or manmade or even a volcanic eruption are, there is nothing more frightening than being eaten alive by a horde of zombies. These rules have been created to ensure that you will not end up a pile of blood and bone on the floor.

In the event of a zombie apocalypse nobody actually knows how the government will react, but I'm betting they'll have bunkers, helicopters, weapons and escape plans in place before the news hits the headlines, by which time it will be too late for the rest of us to act.

Mass elimination of towns and cities or containment of towns would take place from borders to quarantine.

Always be one step ahead, keeping your guard up and your wits about you. Spend less time playing video games on your smartphone and more time keeping an eye on events and news for any sign of the impending zombie apocalypse. Keep a log book of events and the news.

If you are lucky enough to be reading the book before the zombie apocalypse then always look out for the signs. Always watch the news and scan the internet, if you see a pattern or a mysterious pandemic which is striking across the globe then it is time to take action, though you should be prepared at all times. Always have your bug-out bag at the ready with your cupboards stocked with food, water and other essential supplies. Always live in an ABC state:

A- Is for action

B- Is for be prepared for the zombie apocalypse

C- Is for caution

C- is the state you should be living in at all times, be cautious no matter what. Learning these rules and changing the way you live will ensure you are prepared. Start adding items for your defense, food supplies first aid and clothing.

Before the zombie apocalypse hits always be prepared. If you are going to visit family or maybe stay over at a friend's house for the weekend, always take your bug-out bag with you. The more survivors, the more hope there is of getting things back to a so-called normal state. Of course after the zombie apocalypse it will be a new world with new rules, laws and new beginnings.

Zombies can't communicate either with other zombies or humans. It may in some cases look as if they are doing so but it will be a lot of zombies all going towards a sound or a smell that is attracting them.

Zombies don't have memories of their former lives.

Zombies may seem to show signs or false attempts to reconnect that may seem as if they are drawn to a person. This would only be a coincidence and seem to the person as if they had some former memory.

Zombies in their normal state cannot be trained and cannot learn as a rule, who knows what will happen in the future with breakthroughs in drugs and testing.

Rule # 1
Always be prepared to bug out day or night.
Remember this rule.
Get your bug-out routine down to a fine art, practice bugging out both during the day and at night, even half way through a shower or dinner. You'll be faster each time. Try to beat your own record.

Rule # 2
Never wear headphones.
When you can't hear what's going on around you, you leave yourself open to attack. Don't find yourself on the street, jiving along to your favourite tune, only to find you've walked straight into a horde of zombies.

Rule # 3
Keep down. Keep out of sight and keep on moving.
Remember these rules when traveling at all times.

Rule # 4
Fill a bathtub with water.
As soon as pandemonium strikes, fill your bathtub with water and fill any bottles or saucepans.

Rule # 5
Destroy the staircase
If you have to, gather all your supplies upstairs and then destroy the staircase. Make sure you have rope or a rope ladder for when you want to get down. Only do this in an emergency, no other escape plan, situation.

Always secure all the downstairs windows and doors. Add wood and any other barricade materials to the windows and doors. You can also set up traps or place nailed boards under windows. They will get a nasty shock when they come in, slowing them down enough for you to be able to move fast if you have to.

Rule # 6
Don't go back for anything
Keep moving forward. Don't be tempted to dash back to retrieve that precious keepsake. This is when accidents happen.

Rule # 7
Keep fit!

Keep fit and active. Keeping fit is essential to surviving the zombie apocalypse as you will need to outrun the walking (or in some cases speed-walking) dead; let's just hope it's not a rage virus with super-fast zombies. You may need to outrun a whole horde of zombies, you may need to run to get your weapon/supplies, rescue a friend/relative or from other survivors. You need to increase both the fitness levels and stamina of your body. Start a daily fitness routine and stick to it, your life may depend on it.

Whatever your current state of fitness, start keeping fit, it is essential to your survival. Don't underestimate this one. It will be dog eat dog out there. Start implementing a daily fitness routine lasting at least thirty-five minutes a day.

Remember this rule, you will find ways of keeping fit throughout this book. Don't put yourself at risk of getting bitten by a zombie or being an easy target for other survivors. KEEP SAFE-KEEP FIT.

Rule # 8
Mental preparation

Being mentally prepared is essential. When the zombie apocalypse arrives be prepared to kill both the dead and the undead. You may need to kill survivors if your life is in danger and if the shit hits the fan, be prepared to kill friends or family in the event that they have turned into the walking dead.

Try not to get emotionally involved with new members of the group; you may need to dispose of them if they turn. Get yourself ready for anything, expect the unexpected. It's time to get yourself ready to tackle any obstacle that may come your way.

Rule # 9
Have an attitude for survival

You have no option but to survive, you owe it to yourself and your family.

Keep an attitude of survival. You will be forced to do things that the former you would have never dreamed of doing, but remember, you are living an entirely different life now and you will do anything you can to help your chances of survival. Release the inner marine in you, you are strong, you were born to be a survivor.

Rule # 10
Trust no one

This may sound strange, and of course I don't mean your husband/wife, but when meeting fellow survivors it can be risky. Don't let your guard down and keep your wits about you. Although a larger group can mean a greater chance of survival, be wary until they have earned their place in the group. They may try to steal everything you have and even kill you. Trust no one; after all, you are a survivor.

Rule # 11
Destroy the Brain

You have to destroy the brain of the zombie in order for it to be properly dead. Be prepared to do this as you really won't have a choice when it comes to protecting yourself and your loved ones.

Rule # 12
You are never truly safe

Even when you think that you're safe, you are not. Never let your guard down. Don't get too relaxed, you will never be truly safe.

Rule # 13
You will have to fight

You will have to fight, there's no getting away from this. You will need to fight zombies and possibly even wild animals. You will fight people bigger and stronger than yourself. You will need to use what you can to your advantage; weapons, surroundings and of course your brain.

Rule # 14
Always carry a weapon

Use weapons at your disposal, these may be guns, machetes, crowbars, knives, shovels or fire extinguishers. Whatever weapon you have, carry it with you at all times. This will save your life and help you survive the zombie apocalypse. See your weapon as an extension of your new self.

Rule # 15
Safety in numbers

If you are in a safe group of people that you know and can trust, don't leave them, even if the majority of the group wants to go one way and you the other. You have will have a greater chance of survival in a group than on your own, remember this.

Rule # 16
Always have an alternative escape route

This is a must! You may have to go in search of supplies into your nearest town or even an unknown town; you may get cornered unless you have an alternative escape plan. Think smart.

Rule # 17
Wear protective headgear

It's advisable wherever possible to wear protective headgear. Anything which can prevent a bite to the face or head is ideal, but don't choose anything which may obstruct your vision or impair hearing. Headgear is ideal if you are entering a high-risk situation.

Rule # 18
Always wear tight clothing

You don't have to wear a leotard but wear tight clothing, no baggy jeans with your pants showing. Fashion, I'm afraid, will be long gone in the event of a zombie apocalypse and practicality will take over. Safety first here, loose clothing is easily caught, which can prevent you escaping from a situation where you don't have time to spare to unhook caught-up clothing, it can literally mean the difference between life and death.

Rule # 19
Collect weapons

Your new hobby is to collect weapons. You can't go online and buy weapons but on your travels you can add to your weapons.

When you're walking carry more than one weapon on you. Don't rely on just one weapon as it might fail just when you need it most. When walking try to have at least 3 weapons at the ready at all times, remember to learn how to use your weapons safely.

Rule # 20
Protective clothing

Think protective clothing. Layer up wherever possible, making it difficult for zombies to take a chunk out of you. If you can obtain a bullet proof vest this may save you when under attack from other survivors. Waterproof and warm clothing are a must, you can't afford to catch a cold or flu, making you weaker and unable to protect yourself.

Rule # 21
Water is the most precious commodity

In a survival situation water will quickly become one of the most precious commodities, so store water as much as you can. Be sure to keep hydrated, by this I don't mean guzzle all of your remaining water. Use your water wisely, spread it out, but you must keep hydrated especially if you are out in the sun a lot. Always be on the lookout for more water supplies. Not getting enough water will cause your body to dehydrate leading to energy loss, dizziness, fatigue, constipation and even cystitis. Use this tip when you need to hydrate quickly.

To a litre bottle of water add half a teaspoon of salt and one teaspoon of sugar then give it a shake; this will aid rehydration when you need it most. Always carry water with you and always be thinking of sourcing more water.

Rule # 22
Learn to make Molotov cocktails

The Molotov cocktail is an important part of your survival; it is versatile and very effective. A beer bottle full of flammable liquid with a handkerchief soaked in paraffin as a lighting device is ideal. You can use this against many zombies at a time.

Rule # 23
Do not eat the zombies

This may come as a no brainer but there will be times when you are ravenous yourself and could literally eat anything and even the walking dead may look like a walking cheeseburger, but don't attempt to eat their flesh either uncooked or cooked.

Rule # 24
Eat sensibly

By this I don't mean your five a day packed with fruit and veggies, but ration your food and make sure if you are walking for long periods of time that you refuel your body and at regular intervals.

Rule # 25
Never Keep Zombies as Pets

It's not only inhumane but they may attack you or other people and attract other survivors or zombies. These are vile, disease-carrying, germ-ridden beings that you certainly don't want near you, so think on.

Rule # 26
Learn to drive

There is no better time to perfect your driving skills than in the event of a zombie apocalypse, not being able to drive in this kind of situation is out of the question. Should you be unable to drive when the apocalypse strikes you will have to learn the hard way (better to be prepared). There will be times when you will need to be able to drive. If you are in a group of people and one of you can drive, teach the others. You can't rely on one person, they may be eaten alive by zombies and then there's no driver. If you are on your own, practice carefully whenever possible, it could save your life.

Rule # 27
Make your own weapons

With the right tools you can make a weapon from most things. You may be stuck indoors but one of the first things you should do is equip yourself with as many weapons as you can find. Knives, screwdrivers and other household tools are fantastic. Even old bricks can be used as weapons to throw at zombies. Broken glass, broken furniture legs and power tools are all great weapons. Tying knives and other weapons to broom handles is also ideal.

Rule # 28
Start making plans for your future

In the event that an apocalypse-type situation takes place, you will need to be planning ahead for your future.

Ok, so things will be different now. You won't be able to put money by for Friday-night pizza and movie nights but plan your food and drink rations as best you can.

Choose a destination, maybe you want to get to an island, a pier or even a large boat. Start planning now. If you wander endlessly without a goal you will eventually succumb to the zombies.

Rule # 29
Don't keep rotting bodies near your base

This one's important. Don't keep rotting dead bodies in your base even if you have personal attachments to the deceased, you cannot do a Norman Bates here. Burying the dead is ideal but only if you are in a place where smoke and fire will not attract more zombies. If you cannot burn the bodies at least move them far away from where you are or bury them.

Rule # 30
Learn martial arts

In the event of an apocalypse, being equipped with the knowledge of protecting yourself is the greatest weapon. You don't have to be like Bruce Lee or get a black belt in karate but it is important to learn martial arts skills. Practice punching and kicking. A rolled-up mattress taped together makes for a great makeshift punch bag. Practicing in pairs allows you to be on the attack and the defense.

Rule # 31
Stock up on food and drink

This one's obvious but you would be surprised at how many

people forget to ration their food. In the event of an apocalypse food will keep you strong. You need to know where your next meal is coming from or just how long your rations will last. Prepare, keep the cupboard stocked with things to bulk up on, such as rice and pasta which will fill you up and is cheap and convenient to stock up on and keep just in case you should ever need it.

Food and drink will become the new currency and if you have prepared and have plenty of stored food not only will you be able to stay alive but you will be able to trade food for other things you may need. Keep a checklist so you are aware of exactly what you have and try to store tinned foods as they have a long shelf life and will be able to keep you going for a long time. Use a special cupboard in your kitchen for these foods and don't allow yourself to dip into them unless the apocalypse has begun. The end of the world won't wait if it ends on your weekly shopping day and you have nothing in.

Rule # 32
Board up all doors and windows

Securing your home is very important, do this well and as long as you are stocked up on food you will be able to stay in the confines of your home for as long as possible. This will be the safest place to be. Use any available wood, breaking up tables, doors, wooden furniture and nailing them to windows and doors. If you are well-prepared you may not have to leave your house for some time, and if no zombies can get in you will have a greater chance of survival.

Rule # 33
Use your loft

If you have one use it. If you have a loft, keep some of your supplies there. If you have everything you need in there you can cut yourself off from the rest of the world, closing the loft hatch behind you. To be on the safe side make sure you have a window or a way out if the shit hits the fan. Best to take a rope ladder with you in case you have to climb down from the building.

Rule # 34
Only shoot if you have to.

By this I mean the gunshot will alert other survivors and possibly hordes of flesh-eating zombies. If you can safely get out of the situation using another weapon then do so.

Rule # 35
Sleep upstairs

If the house is secure chances are you'll be safe. However, should zombies or other survivors get into your home whilst you're sleeping upstairs, you will have more chance of being woken before anyone gets to you. If you have locks on the doors in your home, keep the bedroom locked at night as an extra preventative. A great tip is to remove the stairs/partially remove the stairs (where applicable) using a ladder instead. This way you can haul the ladder up when you are upstairs, preventing anyone or anything else coming up.

Rule # 36
Medical supplies

Stock up on medical supplies. Things like aspirin and paracetamol, even down to medical supplies like hay-fever tablets nasal sprays and eye baths could be needed and if you stock up on these bartering is always an option. If you are on long-term prescription medication try to put in a repeat prescription slightly early each time so that you have some spare should you need them, the pharmacy may only be round the corner but if the world ends this will be the first stop for lots of survivors and you may run the risk of having to go without.

Rule # 37
Keep lights off

When it's dark keep lights off so as not to alert anyone to your location. A dark house will look unoccupied but a light on will send out a signal to both infected and survivors to come in. Use dull lighting in rooms of your home where the windows and doors are well boarded. You can also nail sheets up over the boards to stop any light escaping. You will obviously need light when you are preparing food and such, but keep it to a small candle and keep in the dark as much as possible.

Rule # 38
Always sleep with your weapons close by
This may sound obvious but it is important to always sleep next to your weapon or weapons. When you wake up with a jump (when someone calls in the middle of the night) you can be disorientated and unable to find your weapon. If it's right there next to you, you will have a chance to defend yourself before being attacked.

Rule # 39
Always aim for the head
As we know from numerous zombie movies, body shots are a waste of time and ammunition. Whether you are shooting or hitting with a hammer always go for the head or you will be just wasting time and energy.

Rule # 40
Cover all wounds
It's important to cover any wounds or open cuts that you have

on your body or that people you are traveling/staying with have on them. The smell of fresh blood is very attractive to the undead. Think safety, keeping your wounds covered will be more hygienic and lessen the chances of you getting infected.

Rule # 41
Don't run with your knife

This rule may save your life, remember your mum always saying don't run with scissors or knives? Well there's a lot of common sense there, if you are running and carrying a knife at the same time always face the blade downwards or away from you. You would be surprised at how many people make this mistake and in this situation it could cost you your life.

Rule # 42
Wear a survival vest

This will depend on availability or where you can obtain or steal one from but as soon as possible get one. If you are out and cannot carry a rucksack due to carrying or collecting other items, a survival vest with lots of pockets and pouches is ideal to carry your pocket knives, ammo, and some first-aid essentials.

Rule # 43
Cover your tracks

Cover your tracks, don't lead anyone to you. You can even make false tracks to confuse other survivors. Your tracks can easily give you away so carry a long stick and use it to sweep over your tracks as you go.

The last thing you want is to lead other survivors to your base.

Rule # 44
Camouflage

Camouflage is very important, you not only have to be undetectable to zombies but you will also need to be undetectable to other survivors who will be trying to steal your food, water, clothing and anything else they can get their hands on. Ok, so you can't pop down to the local army surplus shop but use your surroundings, in woodland areas use branches, twigs, ferns and mud to disguise yourself.

Rule # 45
Eliminate zombies

It sounds obvious but every one that you kill is one less that will bother you later on. It may seem like an endless battle but do what you can to keep the number of zombies in your area to a minimum.

Rule # 46
Don't miss

When you aim at a zombie try to hit it, don't miss, especially if you only have one bullet left in your gun.

Rule # 47
Kill anyone who shows signs of becoming infected

This is imperative, be vigilant and kill anyone who shows signs that they are turning. This rule may save your life.

Rule # 48
Use a knife with a good grip

It's important that the knife which you carry with you as part of your survival equipment has a good grip and won't fall from your hand. You can use a parachute cord or rope, and leave a loop big enough as a handle, think of a Wii remote cord, you want to be able to fight without losing a grip on your knife.

Rule # 49
Acquire a slingshot

These are an important accompaniment to the zombie apocalypse survival kit. You can use these to smash windows from a distance and to confuse zombies by making a sound in a different direction than the one you are heading for. A slingshot can also be used for defense and for hunting.

Rule # 50
Keep your hair short

You don't see many boxers or fighters with long hair. This is for a good reason. It is safer to have short hair, long hair can be grabbed at, get caught up, and block your peripheral vision putting your life at risk. This goes for men women and children. A shaved head is ideal.

Rule # 51
Gratitude

This may be hard, and yes for most people their family and friends have turned into rotting, walking and eating corpses, and their homes have turned into urban wastelands. Be grateful for your survival when hundreds of thousands of people across the globe haven't. You are a survivor, you are alive, you are a fighter, be grateful for that, this will give you a new outlook on your life.

Rule # 52
Learn to be a Liar

Learn to be a very convincing liar, you may need to lie your way in and out of situations. Don't get caught, practice being convincing, this may save your life some day.

Rule # 53
Store candles

Candles are a fantastic source of light and last for a long time, however, candles are no use whatsoever unless you have a lighter/matches. Candles could also be used for bartering.
If you manage to stay in your home for as long as possible with windows and doors boarded up, you will need some light. Remember to stock up on candles and keep them in a safe dry place.

Rule # 54
Do thirty pushups daily

Thirty, why thirty? Well, thirty is a great number; ten is too small and twenty is ok but easily do-able. Thirty pushups daily will improve your physical stamina helping you fight off zombies should you need to. This will help with your overall fitness.

Rule # 55
Do one hundred sit-ups daily

In your quest for overall fitness and to help defend yourself against the undead one hundred sit-ups a day will increase your physical ability and stamina. Remember, the better shape you are in, the more chance you have of survival and that is the name of the game.

Rule # 56
Get some Earplugs

You may need earplugs to sleep. The undead aren't renowned for being quiet. Listening all day and night long to the cries and screams of dead/dying people is disturbing and you could end up going crazy. Using earplugs is only ideal if you have at least one other person with you on watch. You cannot afford to block up one of your warning devices if you have no one else to alert you.

Rule # 57
Pretend to be a police officer

In certain situations, to calm and assist, pretend to be an officer of the law or a figure of authority. It is ideal to have a back story to make it more believable.

Rule # 58
Try to cover up the rotting smell

Aftershave/deodorants and air fresheners are ideal.
This may sound like the last thing you would need but the smell of rotting flesh and corpses is disgusting, you will need something to cover the stench.

Rule # 59
Get some Caffeine

Coffee is a great stimulant. It tastes good and is great for keeping you alert during the night should you be on look out. Most homes will have coffee so it shouldn't be too hard to find and will be useful when you need warming and perking up. If you can't get hold of coffee try to acquire some caffeine pills or a good strong cuppa.

Rule # 60
Run for twenty-five minutes daily

I call this one the running machine. I'm lying, it's standing on the spot and pretending to be on a running machine and running. Do this for twenty-five minutes plus, daily, to improve your stamina and overall fitness.

Rule # 61
The squat

The squat will improve your overall fitness, each of these exercises preparing your body for enduring pain, strengthening and lengthening your muscles to better your chances of survival.

Rule # 62
Acquire a whistle

A whistle is a great tool to have; you can use this as part of a group to signal to other members without attracting too much unwanted attention. You can work out a code between the members of the group, for example one means stop, two means go, three means abort mission etc. This is a very useful communication tool to have.

Rule # 63
Head for high ground
Try to head for high ground as this will give you an advantage; always be able to see your surroundings.

Rule # 64
Meditate
Meditation is very useful as this will help you to de-stress and give you a positive outlook on things. Be sure to meditate only when you are 100% safe. I suggest having someone on guard.

Rule # 65
Play a game
Try to have time when you play games, charades, give us a clue or I-spy a zombie is a great way to pass the time.

Rule # 66
Read

Read anything you can, learning from books is a great way to pass the time, you never know what skills you might pick up that could come in handy.

Rule # 67
Get Yourself a Map

Get yourself a map of your area and surrounding areas, cities, etc. The bigger the better as you won't know until the apocalypse happens just where you will need to be headed. An A-Z is great. This item will increase your chances of survival greatly, so don't forget to equip yourself with this now.

Rule # 68
Quarantine any survivors who may be infected

It is important to quarantine any fellow survivors who may be a risk to you, even if they have been bitten and you have managed to quickly remove the limb (which hopefully would prevent the virus spreading) it is important to keep them in quarantine for at least twenty-four hours, preferably forty-eight hours.

Rule # 69
Grenades

If you are lucky enough to be able to get your hands on grenades don't waste them. They will be hard to come by, so if you do have grenades only use them in a life or death situation. Be aware that grenades would not necessarily kill zombies as you have to destroy the brain directly.

Rule # 70
Smelling salts

Try to make smelling salts part of your apocalypse preparations. You will need them for yourself and possibly other people. There will be plenty of blood and gore come the end of the world, also low blood sugar from dietary deficiencies may cause fainting.

Rule # 71
Chew gum

Only chew sugar-free chewing gum. This will help with your dental hygiene, and you do see commanding officers chewing gum so there's got to be something in it.

Rule # 72
Never get emotionally attached

To a zombie or a fellow new survivor. Your emotions may be your downfall and may make you let your guard down and think differently, putting yourself and others in danger.

Rule # 73
Cereal bars

Cereal bars are an awesome form of nourishment. When you run out steal as many of these as you can, they will keep you going strong for hours.

Rule # 74
Learn languages

Get others to teach you new languages. Learning a new language from a member of your team will be a great asset to you, especially when encountering other survivors.

Rule # 75
Goggles or protective eyewear

Goggles are a great idea. Think like a mad scientist or a steam-punk enthusiast. If you can get your hands on them, they will prevent blood splatter going into your eyes.

Rule # 76
Get a gun

It will be your best and most valid weapon. It will save your life and the lives of others around you. It will allow you to kill those pesky zombies without getting too close. Try to acquire a gun but don't put your life at risk to get it.

Rule # 77
Play dead

Playing dead can really work in your favour; this can work out great in a zombie or survivor raid. Use playing dead to your advantage.

Rule # 78
Acquire a Bicycle

The mountain bike is a great tool for traveling over all different types of terrain, especially when trying to avoid towns.

Rule # 79
Be a silent assassin

Try to acquire a silencer for your gun, this may save your life as any noise you make will most definitely attract zombies and survivors to you, the quieter you are the less chance you have of being eaten alive or killed by other survivors.

Rule # 80
Keep a diary

Keep a diary account (if you can), this will help other survivors know of your findings and may just keep you sane.

Rule # 81
Don't run into danger

When you are running you can get yourself into dangerous
situations, quickly turning a corner could reveal there are
hundreds of zombies in every direction.

Rule # 82
Don't touch zombies

They're full of disease and germs. Where possible avoid
physical contact with them at all costs.

Rule # 83
Boil water before drinking it

If you haven't got any water purification tablets be sure to boil
water before drinking it. You can then drink it warm or leave it
to get cold before drinking.

Rule # 84
Don't get bitten

Do not let yourself be bitten by a zombie. If you do it is game over or at least a limb missing if you are very lucky.

Rule # 85
Be a leader

If the situation arises, elect yourself as a leader. Don't be a follower. Be a leader, show your skills and knowledge and self-worth to the group. Don't follow someone else into death.

Rule # 86
Don't play with Zombies

Ok, it may be tempting to have fun with them, race them, use their heads as bowling balls, etc. but it will only end in tears. Don't take chances, just don't do it.

Rule # 87
You can't hang a zombie

Remember this, don't even waste your time trying, they will not die from hanging so don't break your back trying to find this out.

Rule # 88
Decapitate and then destroy the brain

This may be easier said than done but decapitating a zombie then destroying the brain is ideal.

Rule # 89
There may never be a cure

Don't kid yourself, be prepared. There will probably never be a cure for this and the chances of you getting a cure are slim to none.

Rule # 90
Share your skills and learn

Share the skills you have with others and vice versa. Learn from each other. If one of you can tie great knots and one is a great huntsman, teach each other your skills. Be sure to learn and share, this may just save your life.

Rule # 91
Try not to think about takeaways and fast food

Try not to think of buckets of chicken or your favourite Chinese take out. A good way of doing this is to think of zombie's guts whist pretending to eat it. Do this a few times and every time you think of take-away it will repulse you.

Rule # 92
Teeth

No, not zombie teeth but yours, keep them clean where you can along the way. Brush your teeth, there will be no dentists and it is important to look after your teeth.

Rule # 93
Shit hits the fan

When the shit hits the fan have an escape plan and route and be sure to have your bug-out bag at the ready. Don't trust the government or the army, this may sound strange but they may lead you to your death or force an untested vaccine on you.

Rule # 94
Expect cell/mobile phones not to work

Plan meeting places with friends and family in advance, a designated meeting place that is away from the city. Cell phones will be down. Know this now and plan ahead.

Rule # 95
Make an escape plan

Plan to evacuate the city at the first sign of any danger. Practice and practice again. Plan your route in daylight and at night. Try to go undetected by anyone looking for places of cover along the way.

Rule # 96
Weight train

Make your own weights using tinned goods or other items from around your home. It's important to keep strong. You will need every ounce of strength you can muster to see this one out.

Rule # 97
Learn how to hunt

Know how to hunt and be prepared to hunt. You can do it, be quiet, be fearless and be ready.

Rule # 98
Head away from towns and big cities

There is always a big risk that towns and big cities may get destroyed by the government first. Also, there will be many survivors looting and killing and hordes of the infected.

Rule # 99
Acquire a Bandana

Always have a bandana on you. This will come in handy for putting over your nose and mouth for covering up bad smells/disguising yourself and even to tie hair, sweatband, ideal for blocking the sun from your neck, a sling, washcloth, tourniquet, cleaning toll and dust mask.

Rule # 100
Celebrate

Continue to celebrate your birthday, Thanksgiving and Christmas. Go for it! Why should those evil zombies ruin your day?

Rule # 101
Sleep in trees

You can sleep in trees and/or hide in them. Use trees to your advantage. If you find that you need to sleep in a tree, tie yourself with rope, securing yourself. Otherwise it could go very wrong indeed.

Rule # 102
Round up zombies like cattle

Maybe you are trying to free an area from zombies. Think like a cowboy rounding up cattle, a bigger target is an easier one. Be careful only do this in large groups and if you have to. I suggest having some good fire power with you if you do.

Rule # 103
Keep a calendar

You should always use calendars. Note down the date, it may help you prepare for the elements if you know when the next season is coming.

Rule # 104
Get some Running shoes

Acquire a decent pair of running shoes/trainers. You won't outrun a zombie or a bloodthirsty survivor with a pair of high heels or cowboy boots. Trainers and running shoes are also great for stealth so enemies won't hear you coming.

Rule # 105
Samurai sword

Admittedly if you don't own one of these it might be difficult to acquire, however, these are used for decorative purposes and if you happen to have one, use it to your advantage. These are great when used in close contact. Who will mess with you with one of these to hand?

Rule # 106
Know your enemy

It's good to know your zombies and know exactly what you're up against. Watch them from a safe distance and work out exactly how they move, what alerts them, how fast they are, etc., or if they have any weaknesses you can use in your favour.

Rule # 107
Protect your glasses

If you need glasses to see then they are vital to your survival. Wear protective goggles over them to prevent them from breaking. Remember the opticians won't be open for business so look after your specs.

Rule # 108
Blend in

Whatever situation may arise, try to ensure you blend in as much as possible. When meeting new survivors don't be too opinionated and cause any friction until you are well-adjusted into the group.

Rule # 109
Acquire a crowbar

Get a crowbar, it's the perfect defense weapon against zombies.

Rule # 110
Acquire a machete

Get a machete, they are great for close contact and all round zombie killing.

Rule # 111
Don't wear high heels
It's obvious really isn't it?

Rule # 112
Pad your self as much as possible
Foam or polystyrene, either of these can be used to pad your body underneath clothing, making it harder for zombies to get to your flesh, as this will act as a barrier. Most duvets are made of this kind of material which can be broken down, cut to size and wrapped around the body before putting on clothing.

Rule # 113
Always keep your distance from the undead
This may sound obvious but distance is key. Build your base away from zombies, store food and supplies out of sight and with enough distance from the undead. Think of distance when building parameters.

Rule # 114
Get a utility belt

Get yourself a utility belt, if you don't own one you can improvise with rubber bands, rope and cord.

Rule # 115
Build a tree house

If you find that you have the time or time is on your side build a tree house as a temporary base. Use a rope ladder and don't forget to pull it up after you. Use bushes and leaves to camouflage it well from other survivors and the infected.

Rule # 116
Practice head shots

Whatever else you do, practice your head shots. Use a watermelon or similar item to practice your headshots as much as possible.

Rule # 117
Quit Smoking

Try to cut down smoking, not only will you need to, but you should try to quit altogether to get you at your peak fitness.

Rule # 118
Acquire rubber gloves

Get yourself a pair of rubber gloves, the stronger the better. They are fantastic for keeping your hands sanitised because you will be touching some weird shit, trust me.

Rule # 119
Make a shield

Try to make a shield. There are lots of things you can use for this but use your initiative and use what's around you. The police have shields for a good reason, it will help protect you from attacks. An obvious one is to use the lid of a metal dustbin, and you'll be Captain Survivor!

Rule # 120
Hide a knife in your socks/boots

Try to keep a concealed knife on you, that way if you are captured by other survivors you will be able to get free and protect yourself from them. Make sure the knife has a cover so you don't injure yourself.

Rule # 121
Set up a rationing system for food and drink

It is important to set up a rationing system, always check what you have left in supply and what you are eating.

Rule # 122
Acquire some combat boots

Try to obtain a pair of combat boots, ensuring that the laces are always tied and tucked away to prevent tripping. Combat boots are one of the best pieces of kit and if they are steel-capped even better.

Rule # 123
Go to the toilet in pairs

Yes, women all over the globe had it right all along. Going to the toilet in pairs could save your life, one person should always be on guard.

Rule # 124
Stay off drugs

Don't take any drugs, they may impair your reaction time. I don't mean an inhaler or some aspirin but recreational drugs. Mind-altering drugs are a definite no no. Not only are they unsafe but you may see things that aren't really there; you might shoot your buddy thinking he's a zombie.

Rule # 125
Acquire a Leather jacket

Get yourself a leather jacket. Leather is very strong and durable, it can fight the elements and may help pad against a bite.

Rule # 126
Two-door car rule

Try to ride shotgun when you are unable to drive. Never go in the back seat of a two-door car. If there is an accident this will leave you vulnerable to attack while unable to exit the vehicle.

Rule # 127
Learn how to hot wire a car

It is important to learn how to hot wire a car, this is a must. You will be able to get out of many situations with your newfound skill.

Rule # 128
Knowledge is power

Read as much as you can, the more you learn, the more skills you will have. Learn from books, friends and other survivors.

Rule # 129
Don't make silly mistakes

Don't make silly mistakes, this is a great rule. Think and
rethink everything you do.

Rule # 130
Always check that they are dead

This is very important. Always check that the zombies are dead.
Check and check again. Do this every time you kill one and it
will become second nature.

Rule # 131
Don't let yourself get depressed

Don't let the word depression be part of your vocabulary, stay
positive and keep fighting.

Rule # 132
Be alert twenty-four seven

Ok, it will be hard and virtually impossible to be alert twenty-four seven. Do it in a team or if you are on your own try to stay alert as long as possible, even when you are asleep. Always have someone on the lookout twenty-four seven. Take it in turns with shifts, even if you think you are 100% safe you are not. This will become tiresome but make it a part of everyday, something you have to do like brush your teeth. Take turns at different hours, it works much better the more people there are in the group. Who knows, the late night shift might not come around again for a good few days.

Rule # 133
Power nap regularly

Change your regular sleep pattern and take twenty-minute power naps, ideally every three hours. Power naps are great and after you've used them for a while you will get used to them. When you get a chance you can even have a few hours' sleep and still power nap.

Rule # 134
Hygiene

Hygiene is a must, wash every chance you get (at least daily). You can't afford to let your hygiene go.

Rule # 135
Always Travel with a partner

Try to travel with a partner, even if you are nipping out to get some tools. Get used to doing this.

Rule # 136
Be persistent

You will always get a persistent zombie who will not go down; I like to call them zombienators. Keep going for it, he/she will go down eventually.

Rule # 137
Get ready to Run

Be ready to run, expect to run, this is going to happen. You will have to run from the undead and other survivors.

Rule # 138
Get some Vitamin C

Get some vitamin C. This has many uses, from preventing scurvy to boosting your immune system.

Rule # 139
Slow and steady doesn't win the race

They usually say slow and steady wins the race, but not when running from zombies. Remember this.

Rule # 140
Carry a torch

Always carry a torch. Even if you go out in daylight you never know when you might get stuck and have to hide for a while before making your way back. Carry it ideally in your vest.

Rule # 141
Keep quiet

Always keep quiet; learn to keep quiet, being loud could get you killed.

Rule # 142
Be careful when swimming

Be extra careful when swimming, zombies won't drown. They can't swim but they may be lurking deep in the water, be aware.

Rule # 143
Learn how to use a gun safely

It is important to learn how to use a gun properly, practice using it every day.

Rule # 144
Check the safety is off

This is one thing, one little thing that could save your life. When you are not using your gun always keep the safety on. When you get ready to shoot always make sure you check that it is off.

Rule # 145
Always be confident

Be confident in whatever you do. Be confident in the fact that you will get out alive, and when meeting new survivors.

Rule # 146
Acquire a Swiss army knife

This is a great piece of kit. Carry a Swiss army knife with you at all times, you cannot be without one.

Rule # 147
Practice first-aid training

Keep a small, well-stocked, first-aid kit that you can carry on your person with all the essentials, band aids, plasters, a bandage and sanitary wipes at the very least. Always practice, be prepared for injuries such as broken limbs and cuts or even worse.

Rule # 148
Keep calm and fight zombies

Try to keep your cool and stay calm when fighting. You will have more chance of killing the zombies.

Rule # 149
Always close gates and doors

Always close gates and doors behind you. This will hopefully keep out unwanted zombies and survivors.

Rule # 150
Acquire some handcuffs

Handcuffs are a great idea and can be very useful to keep unwanted survivors away from you and can also be used as bait with something attached to them.

Rule # 151
Go vegetarian

A zombie apocalypse is probably not the best time to be eating random meats. You don't have to go veggie, you can still eat pre-cooked tinned meats but stay away from fresh meat. Don't trust anyone who offers you any so-called steak, it's probably their evil stepmother.

Rule # 152
Never let the zombies win

Never let a zombie get the better of you, you are smarter and wiser and have more skill.

Rule # 153
Never, never, never, give up
Never give up, keep fighting. Keep being a survivor.

Rule # 154
Drink alcohol in moderation
If you are going to drink alcohol, drink it in moderation. Don't get hammered, you can't fight zombies with a hangover, you need to be alert at all times.

Rule # 155
Keep in touch with other survivors
It is important to try to keep in touch with other survivors if you can. That way you can share information and knowledge and learn from each other, having a better chance of survival.

Rule # 156
Disable smoke detectors or alarm systems

It may be an idea to disable any smoke alarms throughout the house; as if they go off they will attract zombies. If you still need to use them, cover them with a shower cap; this will block out some of the sound.

Rule # 157
Always check sheds and garages

You should check sheds and garages for zombies and also food and weapons, take what you can.

Rule # 158
Vantage point

At your base make sure you have a vantage point that you can look out from to see any zombies or survivors approaching.

Rule # 159
Eat little and often
Try to eat little and regularly to refuel your body.

Rule # 160
The fast walk
Learn to walk at a fast pace whenever possible, this will lessen
the likelihood of being followed.

Rule # 161
Relocate to the country
The country and other less-populated places will give you a
greater chance of survival.

Rule # 162
There are no rules; there is no law in place. The only rules that matter are these rules:
Survivors will kill, harm or attack you just for a bite of your

favourite chocolate bar. They will be desperate to protect their family by any means possible.

Rule # 163
Don't waste ammo

Only shoot if it is a 100% necessary. Whatever you do, don't waste your ammo. Your gun or guns will be rendered useless without ammo, so stock up and always keep ammo clean and dry.

Rule # 164
Learn calculus

You may need this for a number of things, from bartering to counting the hordes of the undead that are coming straight towards you.

Rule # 165
Be sure to check vets practices for med supplies

You would be surprised how many animal medical supplies can be used to treat humans. Always be careful when approaching places of high interest.

Rule # 166
Never punch a zombie

A punch will not harm a zombie; they will be straight back up.
Find a weapon that can kill it for good.

Rule # 167
You can live three + weeks without food

You can survive without water for up to three days but last as
long as 3 weeks without food. So if it's a fair hike to re-stock
your supplies, you will make it before you succumb to
starvation. I would not recommend trying either though, this is
information for the z-day apocalypse.

Rule # 168
The weak will not survive

There is no place for the weak in the apocalypse, this is the real
animal kingdom now.

Rule # 169
Be careful of babies giving you away

Be careful of newborn babies giving you away to survivors or zombies. Their crying can put you in danger so try to sound-proof the room as much as you can.

Rule # 170
Don't panic

Easier said than done but this won't help anything. When you panic you make mistakes, mistakes that just may cost you your life.

Rule # 171
Barricades

Only use barricades if you have to. When there is no other option you can make barricades from barbed wire, broken wine bottles and many other things.

Rule # 172
Rig an alarm system

Ok, you might not be great at electrical wiring, but anyone can make a great home alarm system using wire or rope with tin cans or bottles.

Rule # 173
Always be wary of other survivors

Be aware that zombies are not the only ones who may be after your flesh. There may be other survivors who are not only after your belongings, food supplies and weapons but they may be after your flesh too, for a quick barbecue.

Rule # 174
Use anything at your disposal as a weapon

Learn to use anything as a weapon. When push comes to shove you may be forced to use anything to hand as a weapon. Think vases, branches, fire or sand to throw in attacking survivors' eyes. Think in terms of hammers, hatchets, pipes, wrenches, spades, rolling pins and kitchen knives.

Rule # 175
Make sure everyone in your group is prepared to kill

This is a must. Ensure that everyone in your group knows how to and is prepared to kill zombies and other survivors.

Rule # 176
Be prepared for other disasters

It's bad enough the living dead are after you but just when you think it couldn't get any worse, it could! Always be prepared for any natural disaster from earthquakes, floods, tsunamis and more. Trust me, floods and zombies would not be a good mix.

Rule # 177
Have a back-up, back-up plan

You will need to have a back-up, back-up plan, as things can go wrong. The place you are heading for may be swamped with zombies so always have back-up plans.

Rule # 178
Don't set fire to zombies

This is a waste of time. It would take some time to cause any damage to the zombie and in the meantime it will still be coming for you on fire, so change your plan.

Rule # 179
Become an entrepreneur

Bartering is key for survival. Think like an entrepreneur, this way you can acquire food, drink, medical supplies and much more.

Rule # 180
Collect items that you can barter with

Never throw anything away, one man's junk is another mans treasure.

Rule # 181
Text slang speech is dead

Text slang will become obsolete, no lol, m8, cul8r, only the good old Queen's English. I suppose the zombie apocalypse brings some good news.

Rule # 182
Fashion is dead

Don't worry about fashion trends, this is the last thing to worry about. Choose practical clothing all the way.

Rule # 183
Make sure it's a zombie

By this I mean if someone is walking towards you covered in blood don't out right attack. It may be another survivor who has had to defend themselves.

Rule # 184
Prepare to prepare

Always prepare to prepare, make checklists then double check
again.

Rule # 185
Don't follow the crowd

Don't follow crowds. As soon as the z-apocalypse hits stay
away from crowds, in fact go the opposite way if you have to.

Rule # 186
Stay away from sewers and subways

Stay away from sewers and subways. They will be dark, leaving
you vulnerable to attacks from zombies and survivors

Rule # 187
Make the most of natural daylight

Make the most of the daylight hours. Only travel in the

daylight, even if this means setting out mega early.

Rule # 188
Know where you're sleeping before it's dark

Always know where you will be spending the night before the sun goes down. This is very important.

Rule # 189
Don't dawdle

Don't wait around and be vulnerable. Once you have left your home you must keep moving until you find a safe place to stay.

Rule # 190
Avoid pubs and bars

Avoid all pubs, clubs and bars as they will be full of unsavoury survivors and most probably zombies. Don't risk it just for a shot of your favorite beverage, you may end up getting shot or eaten.

Rule # 191
Buddy up

If you are alone, buddy up. Try to get a friend who is a killer
shot and the zombies' worst nightmare.

Rule # 192
Self-defense is the best defense

Be used to fighting, practice with friends, learn how to fight
and train hard.

Rule # 193
Don't swing low

If you are using a baseball bat hit high, never swing low. Only
go for the head all the time.

Rule # 194
Give it all you've got

When fighting, hitting or shooting give it all you've got every time, your life will depend on it.

Rule # 195
Never feed the zombies

You're not at the zoo; don't throw a piece of your newly dead best friend at one of the zombies. Just don't do it!

Rule # 196
Always keep knives sharp

Make sure you always keep your knives clean and sharp, you can't afford for your weapons to let you down.

Rule # 197
Learn to be light on your feet

Learn to be really light on your feet and be able to creep around undetected if you have to.

Rule # 198
Keep your eyes peeled

Always be on the look out for traps laid out by other survivors.
Look out for everything from trip wires to nets and more.

Rule # 199
Use buckets as toilets

You can use buckets as toilets. Just use carrier bags then
dispose of the waste safely, it's odds on that the water won't be
working to flush toilets.

Rule # 200
Nowhere is safe

If you think that nowhere is safe you won't go far wrong.
Expect the unexpected at all times.

Rule # 201
Knives, machetes and baseball bats don't need to be reloaded

Weapons that don't require reloading can be great tools. Reloading your weapon can take precious time whereas the weapons above allow repetitive use without stopping to reload.

Rule # 202
Zombies don't sleep

Zombies don't sleep and are always alert to sound and smells twenty-four seven.

Rule # 203
Be aware of wild animals

The world has been overtaken by zombies but you still need to be aware of animals in the wild, protect yourself and remember that animals may be infected.

Rule # 204
Holy water

Holy water is useless against zombies. Don't waste your time; you may as well just spray them with water. Don't throw water over the zombies either because any water you are lucky enough to have will feel like holy water to you anyway.

Rule # 205
Learn to make traps

Learn how to make traps and how best to use these to your advantage. Dig holes and cover with loose sticks, twigs and branches.

Rule # 206
Learn Morse code

It is important to learn Morse code. You will have to use it along the way, learn it today.

Rule # 207
Have a secret code between your group

Have a secret code between yourself and the other members of the group. This way if you are captured by another group of survivors you will still be able to communicate without giving away your plans to your enemies.

Rule # 208
Food on the go

Ensure the food you travel with is high energy and lightweight.

Rule # 209
Always carry a small mirror

This is handy for signaling to other survivors and for use as a code to other members of the group when you are in the thick of it. Foil and even CDs can be used for signaling if you can't get hold of a small mirror.

Rule # 210
S.O.S

The S.O.S signal is three short flashes three long flashes then a further three short flashes with your mirror from the sun's rays.

Rule # 211
Always have a way out

Wherever you are, always have a way out that is safe.

Rule # 212
Spare weapons

Always have spare weapons. Have three or more weapons on you at all times if you can safely carry them. Spare weapons don't have to be a baseball bat and a crossbow or a machine gun, but easy-to-reach weapons that can be concealed on your body. A good idea is to have leg and arm holsters to put knives in, maybe a large survival knife at the side of your shin and a small throwing knife or two on your arms as back up.

Rule # 213
Never play pranks in the zombie apocalypse
Things could go very wrong for you indeed.

Rule # 214
If you get bitten remove the limb immediately
If you are unlucky enough to get bitten on your arms or legs, you aren't that unlucky because if you were bitten anywhere else you would be mincemeat within minutes. Thank your lucky stars you got bit where you did and amputate immediately just above the part where you were bitten and you may have a chance of surviving. Bite onto something as you perform the amputation!

Rule # 215
Always keep your gun loaded
There can be nothing worse than going to shoot a zombie in a close make-or-break situation only to find the gun wasn't even loaded.

Rule # 216
Wait it out

Be prepared to wait it out. Whether you end up in a relatively safe place or keep traveling, be prepared to wait it out for as long as it takes. This could take years to recover from and get back to some kind of reality.

Rule # 217
Get some chain mail

Think like the old knights of years past, get some on your arms, legs and neck. This may just save your life, though bear in mind this stuff weighs a ton.

Rule # 218
It's a zombie-eat-human world

Now that things have changed always remind yourself that they are after your flesh and they are always a threat.

Rule # 219
Don't get scratched by a zombie

Whatever you do don't get scratched by a zombie. It will most likely end up killing you but may take longer to infect you than a bite. If you get scratched go for the same tactics as if you have been bitten by removing the body part before the infection has time to spread throughout the body.

Rule # 220
Always wipe clean your weapons

Don't bring any blood into your base. Clean off weapons first. Make this a daily ritual.

Rule # 221
No second chances

Remember there are no second chances. Okay, you may come back as a zombie but you only get one shot at normal life.

Rule # 222
Never let the zombies win

Always remember this, never ever let the zombies win.

Rule # 223
Beware of children

You may encounter young children who from behind look innocent enough but if they are infected they are as dangerous as the bigger zombies. But they will be more agile. Don't be afraid to treat them as if they are normal zombies. They are just smaller versions of the walking virus.

Rule # 224
Never cover your body in their skin or organs for camouflage

This is unhygienic; they carry all sorts of germs and diseases. If their blood goes anywhere near you (even a drop) wash it off thoroughly, you may have open cuts or blood may go into your mouth or eyes. Learn to keep away from zombies whether living or dead.

Rule # 225
Pimp your ride

If you do have to use transport such as cars, pimp them out first with barriers, metal fences, anything that will give you that extra protection. You can even add sharpened bamboo or spikes to knock zombies out of the way.

Rule # 226
One bullet rule

Always keep one bullet by just in case! I hope that you never have to use it, but rather that than the crazed zombies devouring your flesh when you are alive.

Rule # 227
Don't be a hero and show off

Whatever you do don't be a hero and show off, this will get you killed. Don't try to impress anyone, stay focused on your own survival.

Rule # 228
You can't reason with a zombie

Remember you can't reason with a zombie (no matter how much you scream at it).Even if it is a family member or a friend or even a neighbor that you have known all your life, it will only end badly. You will be wasting your time and putting yourself and other fellow survivors at risk.

Rule # 229
Don't get yourself backed into a corner

This will get you killed. You will have nowhere to go. Always be on the look out and take note of where you are going. This rule applies down alleys and also sideways. Make a mental note of this so as you are moving you are constantly looking for ways out. Don't enter places that don't have multiple exits.

Rule # 230
Don't back track

Whatever you do don't back track. If you go back there may be zombies or even unwanted survivors. You don't want to get yourself lost and end up walking into either a trap or worse.

Rule # 231
Get used to the sight of blood

You will have to get used to the sight of blood you will be seeing a lot of it, you won't have time to react to the blood and gore which you will inevitably come across during the zombie apocalypse, those split seconds could mean the difference between life and death. Learn not to be squeamish at the sight of blood.

Rule # 232
Use sunscreen

Try to use sunscreen whenever possible. Stay in the shade and avoid being directly in the sun between the hottest parts of the day, which is normally between eleven am and three pm. If you don't have and can't acquire any sunscreen just cover up as much as possible, get a hat, shade yourself under trees or use umbrellas for protection.

Rule # 233
Don't depend on power tools

This rule is very important. You are about to kill a zombie that is heading straight for you and the chainsaw has run out of petrol or power. This rule applies to all power tools and tools that use petrol. Power tools can be an asset, a nail gun would be very handy for making your base safer.

Rule # 234
Acquire a crossbow or bow and arrow

The arrow as a weapon is ideal. It is silent but very deadly. You won't attract zombies using this and you can reuse the arrows. You will have to train and practice using the crossbow or bow and arrow. Don't expect to just pick it up and automatically be a skilled marksman.

Rule # 235
Don't rely on other people

Relying on other people for your own safety may end up getting you killed. It doesn't matter if it is a family member or a fellow team mate, the only person you can truly rely on is yourself.

Rule # 236
Poison is useless on the undead

Remember this rule whether you are using poisonous gas or a

poisonous dart, these will have no effect at all on the undead and will be almost useless. The only thing you may end up doing is putting yourself into danger.

Rule # 237
Assume that all technology will not exist

At the first sign of the zombie apocalypse the Internet and even the phone towers may still be operational but it won't be long before all forms of technology will become a distant memory. If you're lucky enough to find the Internet or phones working at the start of the apocalypse make the most of it by contacting relatives and finding out as much as you possibly can and if there are any safe zones you should be headed to.

Rule # 238
Initiate new survivors

It is important to initiate new survivors to your close-knit group. When a new member joins your team it is important to test them and ensure that they are trustworthy. Try leaving the supply cupboard and exits open. I wouldn't suggest leaving weapons unattended or else the test may go very wrong. Always tell other survivors your plans so that they can guard the exits if the shit hits the fan.

Rule # 239
Know your nose

Get to know certain smells, from poisons to drugs and tainted food or drink. Learn the different smells and know when certain foods are safe to eat or not, this applies to food that has gone bad also. Using your nose could save your life.

Rule # 240
Carry a fanny pack/bum bag

These are great for keeping your personal belongings, a survival knife and even small supplies of food and water. A fanny pack will allow you to carry these items conveniently in front of you without compromising your ability to protect yourself, by leaving your arms free. Fanny packs are ideal as they can be hidden under clothing and either worn at the back or front and kept secure by putting through the belt loops on your trousers.

Rule # 241
Be prepared to leave everything behind

The one thing that is the most valuable to you is your life. Be prepared to leave everything you own, even possessions of great sentiment. You may even need to leave your base if it's unsafe, which may mean leaving behind food and water supplies but don't risk losing your life trying to reclaim belongings.

Rule # 242
Do not invade or loot from other groups of survivors

Only do this if it is a matter of life and death. By this I mean if you have run out of food, water, ammunition or if your shelter has been compromised. Try first to reason with the new group, offering them trades either for information, personal belongings you may have or a trade of skills or knowledge. Only attack if you really have to, chances are you won't come out alive.

Rule # 243
Don't leave your base/house when being invaded by looters

This rule is very important. Don't leave your house and go to investigate. Whether you are investigating zombies or looters you will leave yourself open to attack. Survivors who are attacking you won't know how many of you there are. Stay inside and make lots of noise. If you are on your own inside, let the outsiders think there are more. Use dummies, things shaped like heads, music or anything to make the rebel survivors think twice before attacking you. If you see attacking survivors and they haven't seen you, do the opposite. Be as quiet as possible. Try to go undetected.

Rule # 244
Rules aren't meant to be broken

Rules aren't meant to be broken. One of the last rules here is this – don't break these rules. I'm not telling you that you can't bend them slightly to suit your needs and your situation. They may work better in some situations than others but try to stick as close to these rules as possible. It will save your life.

Rule # 245
Learn CPR

Before applying first aid make sure the patient needs it. Lightly tap on the patient's shoulder and speak to them in a slow, clear and concise way. If you get a response there is no need to perform CPR. Apply the appropriate first aid.

If the person is not breathing as they normally should be or even coughing or moving, start chest compressions. Begin by pushing down in the center of their chest twenty to thirty times. Pump hard and fast, make sure the pumps are faster than once per second.

Make sure you tilt the head back and lift the chin. Pinch the nose and cover the mouth, placing yours over it, and begin to blow until you see the chest rise. Give an immediate burst of two breaths. The short burst/breath should last approx one second.

Then continue to administer thirty pumps, followed by blowing. Repeat this step. For as long as you need to.

Rule # 246
Always be on the look out for dangerous creatures

Don't let the fact that zombies are on the loose take away the fact that you may encounter some very dangerous creatures like poisonous spiders, scorpions and snakes. Always be on the lookout, especially when setting up camp. Don't set up your bed for the night on a red ants' nest. If you are well-prepared try to get some insect repellent. Mosquitoes may be carrying the virus so always keep an eye on bites and stings and apply antiseptic creams where applicable.

Rule # 247
Acquire a Parry knife

If you only have one knife in your bug-out bag or with you at all times, make it the Parry blade survival knife. This knife was designed in the mid nineties by Mel Parry from the British S.A.S. The Parry Knife is strong and heavy, the knife has a powerful chopping stroke and has many uses from prying, levering, cutting, whittling, and digging. This knife will cut through almost anything without breaking. It's a good idea to wrap some para-cord around the handle of the Parry Knife, this will not only give you extra grip but you will always be equipped with para-cord for any survival situation. The knife itself measures approx 88" from the hilt to the point and is perfect for general uses and overall survival, protection and defense.

Rule # 248
You can never over prepare

There is no such thing as over preparing, so keep preparing for any situation that may arise. Even if it doesn't you will know that you can handle it if it does, and will survive.

Rule# 249
Don't try to take or loot items from a zombie

The zombie you have just killed may have that pair of sneakers you have been after for the last year or that designer hoodie (with only a few blood stains on it) but don't even think about it! It is far too dangerous to try to acquire items from zombies either moving or dead, their clothing and belongings will also be contaminated with the virus.

Rule#250
Wear a face shield/ mask

This is a simple yet very affective rule. Always wear a facemask where possible, not one that goes anywhere near your eyes but a small one, like a painters dust shield mask. This will stop blood splatter, fumes and airborne viruses.

Rule# 251
Acquire ninja throwing stars

Ninja throwing stars (shuriken) are a great weapon and very deadly if they are handled correctly. The shuriken was once a highly guarded secret in Japan for good reason. You will need to practice using the shuriken. Also be careful when handling and carrying them. They are a fantastic weapon for defense from looters. If an unwanted survivor shows, throwing a ninja star in their direction will be enough to stop them in their tracks. Ninja throwing stars are light and easy to carry but should not be your first weapon of choice against zombies.

Rule#252
Acquire a stun gun

Stun guns or stun batons are great as a deterrent. They easily fit in your pockets and come in a variety of sizes. There is even a large range of them disguised as everyday objects, from mobile phones to small tins. A great weapon for personal security against looters but don't attempt to use it on a zombie or you won't be the only one shaking. Stun guns are great as a back-up weapon but can't be used multiple times without power to recharge.

Rule#253
Get yourself a monkey fist

A monkey fist is a very easy to carry self-defense weapon. The monkey fist is basically rope or para-cord wrapped around a metal ball, normally the ball is around three quarters of an inch and made of steel. The cord can be made adjustable to reach as far as needed. This can be bought and made at home very easily and can be carried on your keychain or just placed in your pocket. The weapon itself looks like a monkey's clenched fist. A knock with this to an unwanted survivor's head could be fatal (don't try to get close enough to a zombie to use it). If you can't get hold of a monkey's fist try making one. A good alternative is placing a pool ball inside a sock and tying the end, making a quick self-defense weapon.

Rule#254
Try to get hold of martial arts knives

Push daggers, tantos and khukris are all great self-defense weapons and make really good back up weapons which can be used in close combat.

Rule# 255
Get an aluminum baseball bat

Aluminum base ball bats are a great weapon against anyone. They give you enough leverage so as to not let people get too close. They are solid and very lethal and easily wipe clean.

Rule # 256
Don't scream

Okay, this rule may sound obvious but people who are exposed to decapitated bodies for the first time or turn the corner only to find a zombie eating someone's brains will instinctively scream. Prepare yourself as best you can and try your hardest not to scream, this will alert zombies and unwanted looters to you.

Rule # 257
Stakes don't work on zombies

They are not vampires. Placing a stake into the heart is useless; it will have no effect at all. It is not ideal to use a stake even when trying to destroy the brain, you would have to get really close to the zombie to drive the stake through its eye socket.

Rule # 258
Car alarms

Car alarms can go off at the slightest touch. If you are hotwiring a car or even looting from the car, be careful and be aware that the car alarm could go off at any minute. If the alarm does go off it will alert zombies and other survivors of your whereabouts.

Rule # 259
Don't exorcise zombies

You may try getting a priest to rid the zombie of its possession. This does not work, is a waste of time and most likely will get you and the priest killed. Zombies will still kill you on holy ground. Hiding in churches and other places of worship is useless. Say your prayers at home and don't travel to worship.

Rule # 260
Look after yourself

From now on you will have to be your own doctor, nurse, psychiatrist and possibly even surgeon. You are now entirely responsible for yourself. Look out for warning signs to take it easy and learn when enough is enough and don't forget to sleep and rest.

Handy hints and tips

Plants for survival

When you have found sufficient shelter, warmth and water you will need a steady supply of food. In most survival situations when food supplies are limited and your stores of tinned goods and other food rations are running low, plants and nature can be a great asset to your food supply.

Nature is ideal to provide you with food packed with nutrients.

Some individuals may be sensitive to certain plants leading to an upset stomach so it's advised to try in small quantities first.

Always ensure you use this guide when eating new plants for the first time to insure they are safe to eat. Many plants can be poisonous and even deadly.

Only test one part of the plant i.e. bud, root or stem.

Always separate the whole plant into sections before use; the root, buds, leaves and flowers.

Hold the plant close to your nose and smell the plant to see if it has a strong acidic odour.

Do not eat any thing for at least eight hours before taking the following tests.

Rub the plant on your wrists and on your elbows waiting for approximately fifteen minutes to see if any irritation occurs. If irritation occurs leave the plant and discard it immediately (do not eat it).

Only drink pure water and the plant you are currently testing, if no irritation has occurred continue with the following tests.

Take a small part of the plant then place it onto your lips. Rub the plant on and around your lips and put some just inside the bottom of your mouth. Wait for up to three minutes. If no irritation (itching or burning) appears, then continue.

Place the plant onto your tongue, holding it there for a further fifteen minutes. If no reaction has occurred then begin to chew the plant but do not swallow at this point. Wait for a further fifteen minutes. If no irritation (itching or burning sensation) occurs, then continue to swallow the remainder of the plant in your mouth.

Wait now for eight hours before eating any more of the plant. If within the past eight hours you have experienced any symptoms of burning, itching or nausea, immediately induce vomiting then slowly drink lots of water, sipping first.

If you have had no side effects then eat a small amount of that part of the plant. If after the following eight hours you are fine and have no side effects then continue to eat the plant as normal.

Be aware that some plants have flowers that are safe to eat but the root or the stem is poisonous. Be sure to test each part of the plant separately in the same way.

Consuming large quantities of certain plants may cause diarrhea, stomach cramps or even nausea.

When eating plants, as a rule, you have to be very careful not to eat any poisonous plants. If they have milky or discoloured sap, thorns, spikes or a bitter taste or an almond scent leave them alone and do not even attempt to eat them. Three-leaved plants or foliage are potentially dangerous. Red or white berries that you don't know are safe can be potentially fatal. Always avoid eating plants that are shaped like beans.

Here is a list of safe plants and berries to eat that you find in common gardens or woodlands.

Clover
Chicory
Dandelions
Chickweed
Fireweed
Strawberries
Blackberries

Prickly pear
Cactus
Plantain
Wild garlic
Onions
Wood sorrel
Green seaweed
Kelp and even laver can be eaten
Wild berries
Blueberry
Gooseberry
May apple
Elderflowers
Mulberries
Apples
Pears
Wild carrot
Wild leeks
Shepherds purse
Cattails
Purslane
Nettles
Lambs quarter/goosefoot
Cooked elderberries are delicious and are full of nutrients.
Burdock root can be eaten but avoid the leaves and tips.

Please only attempt to eat the plants in a survival situation

Avoid eating any wild mushrooms in a zombie apocalypse or at anytime.

If you eat a poisonous mushroom you may not even know until a few days after eating it that it is poisonous. Poisonous mushrooms can badly affect the nervous system and are potentially deadly.

Mushrooms are hard to identify. It is hard to be sure that the mushroom is safe.

General Survival Tips
Pencil and Duct tape

Get hold of some duct tape. Duct tape is an all-round useful tape. This is ideal for sealing windows using polythene or black sacks. It can be used for making weapons, such as taping a knife to a broom to allow you to fight without having to come into close contact with the zombies.

Use this tip when traveling and you can't carry a large reel of tape with you.

Try wrapping a small amount around a pencil. Make sure that the pencil is wooden. You will be able to use shavings from the pencil to start fires, use the lead for writing with and also use the duct tape. Always place a small amount of Blu Tack over the top of the pencil to ensure you don't get injured when traveling.

Common Cattail

Common cattail can be used as a poultice on wounds, bites, boils, burns and even sores. Use the root of the cattail (Native Indians have been using this method for years).

Spice Bush

Spice bush makes a fantastic tea and is great to ward of colds, flu, sore throats and even arthritis. Use the berries from the spice bush to make a tea.

Slippery Elm

Be careful when preparing tea with slippery elm and ensure that you only use the inner bark to make a tea.

Slippery Elm tea is great to help get rid of a sore throat and even an irritated stomach. It is great for clearing away mucous from the body.

Woodlice

Woodlice are great source of natural protein. They can be found in tree bark across the globe.

Peanuts

Peanuts are not only a good source of protein but are packed with calories which is ideal if eaten on long journeys and at times when you need those extra calories.

On the hunt for water

If you find yourself on the hunt for water but can only find dirty water which is unsafe to drink you can still use it in boiling hot conditions. Soak your clothing in the water and wrap the soiled clothes around your head and neck to stop you from losing any more moisture from sweating. This may keep you going for longer, giving you more time to find a drinkable water source.

Leaves for warmth

If you find yourself having to sleep out in the open with no shelter, use leaves and branches to cover yourself. It's a good idea to set out the branches in an apex shape, like a small one-man tent. Cover the structure with extra leaves and branches, then slide in and cover yourself with extra leaves for warmth.

Petroleum jelly

Petroleum jelly can be used as an insulation to cover exposed skin. This will keep you warm. It can also be used as a base for making your own candles (placing a birthday candle in a jar will make it last for hours). Petroleum jelly can also be used as a lip balm.

Onions

Onions can be used as an alternative to smelling salts to help bring someone round.

Insulation

Cardboard, crumpled-up newspapers and magazines can be used as insulation should you find yourself out at night battling the elements.

Splints

If you have to make a splint, make use of newspapers, old magazines and pieces of wood or branches.

Campfires

Be careful when making campfires. Always have at least a three-foot gap between the fire and yourself and be careful as the fire will attract zombies and other survivors.

Jeans

Jeans are a great all-round piece of clothing. They're tough, sturdy and durable. Don't wear flares in case you trip over or leave yourself open to being grabbed at.

Camomile tea

This is great for calming yourself and others. Camomile tea can also help you get a good night's sleep naturally.

Bolt cutters

These are an essential piece of kit that you shouldn't be without.

Clean socks

Try to change or wash out your socks frequently. Don't forget you will be in them quite a bit and you will need them to be in good condition, with foot problems you won't get far.

Fireworks

Fireworks can be used like flares, attracting attention but also zombies. Use them with caution.

Roof tops

Roof tops are ideal places to sleep, and a great viewpoint to plan your best escape route should you need to.

Ak47

Try to acquire an Ak47, and ammo of course (it would be useless without it). This will give you great protection against zombies but use it carefully as gun fire will attract them.

Learn to tie knots

Learn how to tie knots; study them, practice and practice again. This will be very useful for you.

Walking stick/Cane

Walking sticks and canes are very useful for long walks up hills and mountains, relieving you from some of the strain. Also lots of walking sticks have a stiff metal point on the bottom which is ideal as a weapon.

Supermarket

Find a supermarket. You will have everything you will need there. This will be a popular place to hide out so you will have to fight off a few survivors. Be sure to always weigh up the need with the risk factor.

Shave when possible

By 'when possible', I mean when you have a chance. Keep your hygiene up; growing a long beard will open you up for attack by someone grabbing the beard.

Flares

Try to obtain some flares, but use them wisely and only in a situation where you have to as they may attract unwanted attention. Don't count on using flares to be rescued but these could be used as a signal between groups.

Soap
Always carry soap. Liquid soap is ideal but a small bar of soap in a polythene bag will suffice.

Backpack
Always have your backpack stocked with everything you need in case you have to leave in a hurry, which you will most likely have to do. Backpacks are ideal but be careful as a zombie could grab your backpack and put you in danger.

Wheelbarrow
Wheelbarrows are a great way of transporting your belongings or moving your newfound bounty.

Peppermint oil
Peppermint oil can be used as a pick me up, on skin used in carrier oil or used to deter vermin from your base. Use neat on the floor where vermin may get in.

Shopping trolley
Shopping trolleys are good for transportation of food and other items but be aware, some have locks on them when you get just around the corner from the supermarket. Also they can be loud and hard to get up and down curbs.

Using music
You can use car stereos or ghetto blasters as bait, with the music left on and put in a certain place. This will attract zombies and other survivors. Make sure you run quickly away from the car and don't walk straight into the oncoming storm of zombies.

Crank torch

Try to get a crank, wind-up torch battery and save this for emergencies.

Vitamin supplements

If you can get hold of vitamin supplements, get them. No doubt you can't just go to the supermarket and get your 5 a day. You will need supplements to keep your body running efficiently.

Jars

Use jars and screw bottles for drinks. Any leftover drinks can go into these and it will keep them fresh for longer.

Keep your soda fizzy

There is nothing worse in the zombie apocalypse than your favourite soda going flat. After you have poured yourself a glass, shake the bottle vigorously, ensuring that the lid is on. Do this daily and it will keep it fizzy for much longer.

Bay leaves

Bay leaves are great at keeping unwanted cockroaches and other creatures away from you and your belongings. Keep bay leaves in carrier bags and leave them where you are visited by unwanted creatures.

Seeds

Try to get your hands on some seeds; these plants will be your savings for the future.

Protein powder

Try to obtain some protein powder. You can have this with water or juice, which may be hard to get. This will help with your weight training and help you get in tip-top condition ready to fight.

Think of a great memory
No matter what, you will always have your memories, no one can take them away from you. Don't dwell on the past but look forward to a better future.

Shoes with laces
Be careful of shoes with laces, they can easily come undone and trip you up, as well as getting caught and slowing you down. Slip-on or Velcro shoes are perfect.

Dental floss
Oral hygiene is a must and dental floss can also come in very handy for tying things, such as tying branches together to make a shelter.

Wet wipes
Wet wipes are great to keep yourself and your weapons and belongings clean and sanitized. You can use these to clean just about anything and they are a great addition to a first-aid kit. You can wash your face or even use them as toilet tissues.

Barbed wire
Be careful handling barbed wire and climbing over it. Use barbed wire to protect your base from zombies (they aren't keen on it either).

Garlic
Garlic is great. Not only is it a natural antibacterial and can help to stop food poisoning but it will give your immune system the boost it will need in these unsanitary conditions.

Tin opener
If you have stocked up on tinned goods, don't forget the tin opener. You may think you are well-prepared stocking up on

tinned goods but if you can't open them you will only waste energy trying.

Toothache

Toothache still hurts even in a zombie apocalypse. If you have toothache you may very well wish you were dead. Raw garlic and cloves are good at easing the pain and preventing teeth from becoming infected at the roots.

Caffeine pills

Equip your bug-out bag with caffeine pills. Don't take too many of these as it won't do you any good but in situations where you are on your own, or on guard, they will be a great little boost.

Compass

Prepare your bag with a compass; you will need this in your survival kit. This will help you to work out how to get where you want to go. For most survivors, after a period of time, you will need to be on the move. You won't want to be wandering aimlessly and will need a plan of action. Getting to a safe area without a compass will be tricky.

Obtain a saw

Just a small saw will do, but a saw is a must. If you can get a survival commando wire saw, equip yourself with one before the apocalypse begins. If you can't get your hands on the best, any small saw will do. This will be essential for cutting wood for shelters and fires, and also making weapons from wood.

Rope

Always carry a length of rope; this is an important part of your survival kit which has many uses from transporting bodies with rope to securing yourself when climbing out of a window. The more rope you can comfortably carry the better. It will also come in handy for helping to build a shelter.

Water-purifying tablets
Try to get your hands on some water-purifying tablets, these will be like gold dust in the event of an apocalypse and will prove invaluable and a great asset to a survivor.

Chin ups
Try to do chin ups, these are a great upper body strengthener, this will help with your overall fitness too.

Shelter
Always carry tarpaulin and rope. You will need this as a makeshift shelter, or if you get stranded somewhere overnight. It is also handy for use in the trees.

Fishing vest and gear
Convert fishing vests into survival vests; make sure it contains water, first aid, shelter, food and weapons. Look out for other useful fishing paraphernalia to adapt.

Magnesium
Magnesium is great, try to acquire some. This is good for your stomach, also keeping migraines away and preventing headaches and good for asthma.

Cloves
These are great to ward off bad smells; they can also be sucked to take away bad toothache

Make a trash-bag shelter
Should you find yourself out in the elements (not just fighting the zombies), you can make a shelter from a trash bag. Remove the drawstring, cut the bag at the left and right sides and open it

out. Find a wooden stick/branch and run it through the drawstring entrance, then attach one end to a tree and the other to a stake in the ground. This make-do construction will provide a basic shelter from the elements.

Lavender

This is great for de-stressing. Putting a few drops of lavender oil on your pillow or blankets will de-stress you and give you a good night's sleep. Lavender is also great for burns, stings, bites and cuts.

Hot toddy

A hot toddy can reduce symptoms of colds and flu and help with a restful night's sleep. You will need two teaspoons of sugar, a slice of lemon, boiling water and at least 30-50ml of whisky or brandy. Raw ginger, powdered ginger or powdered cinnamon can be sprinkled on top.

Make a scented sachet

Hang a scented sachet in your living space to ward off evil stenches. Cut a chunk of cloth up and put anything you have inside it. Try essential oils, dried herbs, flowers, and add some string and hang to keep the flies away. You can use any cloth.

Collect batteries

Batteries will become a tradable commodity in the event of an apocalypse. They are versatile and with no power will be used to power torches, radios, etc. Don't buy rechargeable batteries and protect your batteries properly.

After sun

Put four used tea bags in some water. Add some mint/mint oil/ lavender/lavender oil, either bathe in or dab on.

Get rid of unwanted smells with some homemade perfume

Here is a great and easy way to make perfume

4fl oz 115ml rubbing alcohol

4 tablespoons whole cloves

Then add any essential oils, 2 drops of lavender is ideal.

Natural skin cleanser

Here is a great natural skin cleanser which you can make up

1 teaspoon milk

1 teaspoon honey

1 tablespoon ground almonds

Peanut butter

You can make your own peanut butter by following this easy guide

200g -300g salted dry roasted peanuts

1– 4 tablespoons of vegetable oil

Season to taste with salt or sugar if needed

Blend/crush or just mix. Place into a clean jar and seal. This will provide a great source of energy for fighting off those zombies.

Keep matches and lighters waterproof

It is important to keep matches and lighters waterproof. Keep them in a plastic baggy or two to protect them from the elements. A lighter and matches are important survival tools.

Worms

You can eat common garden worms. Okay, not by choice but you may have to and it's also easy to make worm farms as a steady source of protein.

Shoe deodoriser

Roll up old newspaper and leave in your shoes or boots

overnight to keep them fresh.

Onion cough mixture

This mixture will sooth a bad cough

2 onions

225ml honey

Lemon juice

Sprinkle of cinnamon powder

115ml warm water

Vodka orange spirit (optional)

Mix the ingredients together. Leave covered overnight.

Stir in the liquid and put in a jar or bottle.

Take 2 teaspoons as needed, no more than four times a day.

Fire Extinguishers

Fire extinguishers and sand are great to have at hand in your base. Learn how to put fire out quickly and safely. Fire extinguishers are ideal if you have a base or are bugging in but not ideal to put in your bug-out bag. Sand is also very handy for putting out small fires.

Credit Card

A credit card is ideal to jimmy locks. It will be useless for any of its former uses.

Hand warmers

Hand warmers give you an instant burst of heat at anytime, though they do wear out quite quickly. They are still a great asset to any survival situation. Normally lasting between three to twenty hours. They can be used to stop your firearms from rusting by putting a used one inside your gun case. They can also be used on aching joints to give relief from pain temporarily.

Laser pointer

A laser pointer can be used to signal for help or even to distract other survivors away from you.

Knuckledusters

Knuckle dusters can be great used to defend yourself against looters and unwanted survivors but are not ideal used at close range against a zombie.

Tips for making a fire

When making a fire, resin from the bark of a pine tree is very flammable and ideal to get a very good fire started.

Survival blanket

Survival blankets are not only good for keeping you warm by reflecting your own body heat directly back to you but they also block out the sun and are made of reflective material. I would suggest packing at least three of these in your bug-out bag, they are lightweight and easy to carry.

Watch with a light on it

Acquire a digital watch with a light on it. Not only will you be able to tell when it's going to get dark or how much time you have but you will also be equipped with a light at all times.

Bug-out bag

The bag in general is solely designed to get you out of an emergency situation. When you buy your bug-out bag make sure it is of high quality and durable. Unless it is of a high quality it may rip and you may end up loosing some life saving gear. Try to buy a nylon bag that is water resistant with foam shoulder straps and ensure that your bag has side pockets so that the weight is evenly distributed throughout. Always make sure the bag has a large capacity.

Water and food are the first things to put in your bug-out bag, you will need to have enough food to last you three – five days at a minimum (if you can carry more easily, do so). MRE meals are ideal being easy to prepare and light to carry. You can buy MRE meals online which are specifically for army use. A gun or any weapon that can be used in long range is ideal for your bug-out kit. You will have to defend yourself against wild animals, looters and most definitely zombies. Don't forget to pack enough ammo for traveling and always carry backup weapons when traveling (knives at the very least).

Red glow sticks would make a great asset to your bug-out bag as they are a great light source.

A sleeping bag is ideal, giving warmth wherever you end up spending the night.

How much ammo do you need? Well who knows how long this will last for. You may be lucky and only have to kill a few zombies. You may be lucky and find a great base with a supply of food and water. On the other hand you may encounter lots of zombies and looters. Ammo is great to barter with. Ensure you have enough ammo in your bug-out bag for a few days, the more you can carry the better. If you are traveling in a group spread the ammo out between you.

Bug-out bag kit (BoB) Basic Guide

The bug-out bag itself

Single-person tent or tarpaulin at the very least.
Items for bartering, gold, silver, batteries and currency just in case!
Sleeping bag
High-protein energy bars for physical activity
Mini portable electric stove
Weapons and ammo
Flares

Night-vision goggles
Needle and thread
Bug Repellant
Lip Balm
Safety Pins
Duct tape
Wet stone to sharpen weapons
Signalling mirror
Iodine tablets
Matches (waterproof if possible)
Magnifying glass
Disposable lighters
Energy drinks
Compass
Caffeine pills
Maps
Swiss army knife
Pen knife
Standard knife
Mallet and tent pegs
Sleeping Bag
Tarpaulin x 3
Binoculars
Water canteen x 2 pre-filled
Parachute cord
First-aid kit (mini with essentials)
Aluminum foil
Bandana
Sunscreen
Crowbar
Axe
Baseball cap
Torch and spare batteries
Mini wind-up torch or solar-powered

Emergency blanket

Whistle

Body warmer

Fishing line and fish hooks

Pepper spray

Diary and pens

Radio and batteries/wind-up radio/solar-powered

Religious items books or charms

Gloves

Tri-fold shovel

Petroleum jelly

Rucksack

Survival knife

Candles

Soap

Towel

Toilet tissue

Tin opener

High-energy foods

Multivitamin

Gas Mask

Flint and steel

Cooking tin

Keep passports and driving licences where you can easily access them

Medication

This is going to be a problem for a lot of people who are on daily medications. Sometimes you can get more than one prescription at a time and safely store. Never stop or decrease meds without advice from your doctor.

Food

When you consider that you need 2,500 calories per day for a man and 2,000 for a woman you will need to plan accordingly, especially as you will be highly active. You will be burning off a lot of calories.

Basic food to store

Always rotate your food; eating the food that is past its sell-by date the soonest

M.R.E.s (Meals Ready to Eat)

Freeze dried meals

All canned or dried goods are great for storing like Baked Beans or Chilli Con Carnie

Water (you will need a gallon per person per day)

Dried meats like beef jerky with good sell-by dates

Peanuts and all nuts in general

Ramen noodles tinned potatoes and sardines

Cooking

A small to medium pot and a large cup to boil water in for both drinking and freeze dried meals.

Salt

Pepper

Garlic power

Chili powder

Cooking oil

Shortening

Baking powder

Soda, yeast

Powdered eggs

Eating utensils

Dried milk

Rice, Wheat

Formula Baby Foods

First Aid Kit

EMERGENCY ITEMS

Basic guide

Spend time learning first aid and how to apply your skills

Painkillers

Hand wipes

Alcohol sanitising gel

Plasters

Adhesive dressings

Tweezers

Digital thermometer

Disposable splinter probes

Scissors

1 standard razor

Sterile cotton gauze swabs

Elastic gauze bandages

Antiseptic wipes

Sterile wound dressings

Tissue

Eye pads

Plastic gloves

Triangular bandages

Crepe bandages,

Saline solution

Survival blanket x 3

Strapping tape

Face shield

Clothing

It's better to be prepared for any climate and adjust when the weather changes so pack your bug-out bag accordingly.

If you are going to be in a cold environment don't forget to wear a woollen hat or balaclava. You lose around 70 % of your body heat through your head. If you find yourself with out a hat, improvise with clothing.

Basic Guide

Poncho
Wide Brim Hat
Camouflage army trousers with side trouser pockets
Cotton shirt, long-sleeved
Combat boots
Running shoes
Short-sleeve shirt
Wool Socks
Rain coat. Waterproof with hood
Sunglasses
Protective eyewear, goggles
Woollen hat
Gas mask
Vests and spare underwear
Leather jacket
Jeans
Body warmer
Vest with pockets and storage space
Balaclava

Never give up, always be ready and keep fighting!

NOTES

NOTES

NOTES

NOTES

COSMIC
EGG
BOOKS

If you prefer to spend your nights with Vampires and
Werewolves rather than the mundane then we publish the books
for you. If your preference is for Dragons and Faeries or Angels
and Demons – we should be your first stop. Perhaps your
perfect partner has artificial skin or comes from another planet –
step right this way. Our curiosity shop contains treasures you
will enjoy unearthing. If your passion is Fantasy (including
magical realism and spiritual fantasy), Horror or Science Fiction
(including Steampunk), Cosmic Egg books will
feed your hunger.

9781782793342